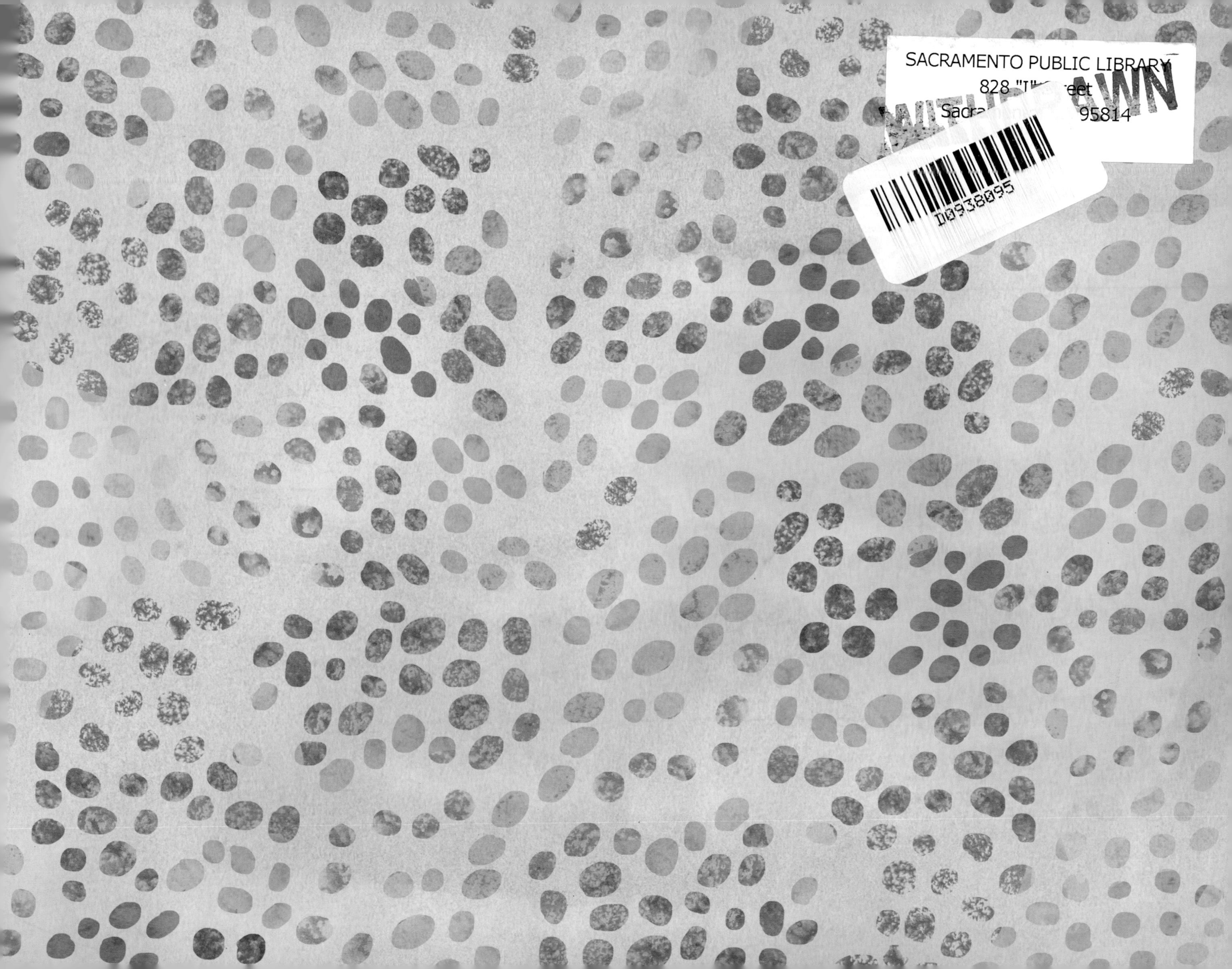

For A, J and J.

An Imprint of Starfish Bay Publishing
www.starfishbaypublishing.com
STARFISH BAY is a trademark of Starfish Bay Publishing Pty Ltd.

COLIN THE CHAMELEON

ISBN 978-1-76036-046-7
Printed and bound in China by Beijing Shangtang Print & Packaging Co., Ltd.
11 Tengren Road, Niulanshan Town, Shunyi District, Beijing, China

Rachel Quarry is an illustrator and artist based in the UK. She studied at Cambridge University and the Cambridge School of Art. In her illustration work she uses ink, monoprint and collage. For inspiration she likes to travel and visit parks and gardens.

Colin the Chameleon

Rachel Quarry

STARFISH BAY CHILDREN'S BOOKS

Colin was a chameleon. His brothers and sisters could change colour to blend into the forest.

But Colin
could not.

'It's not safe to be near Colin,'
said the other chameleons.

So while his brothers and sisters hunted for insects and leaves to eat, Colin hid all day under a leafy branch.

But there was one part of
the forest where no chameleon
was safe.

The chameleons dared not cross the track, though on the other side the insects looked juicy and tasty.

One day Colin leaned too far out from his branch.

STOP!

Colin crawled safely off the track.
Look!

Wait!

'With Colin we can all cross the track!' said the chameleons.
So Colin led the way.
'Hurrah for bright and brave Colin!' they all cheered.

CHAMELEONS
CROSSING
PLEASE DRIVE
CAREFULLY

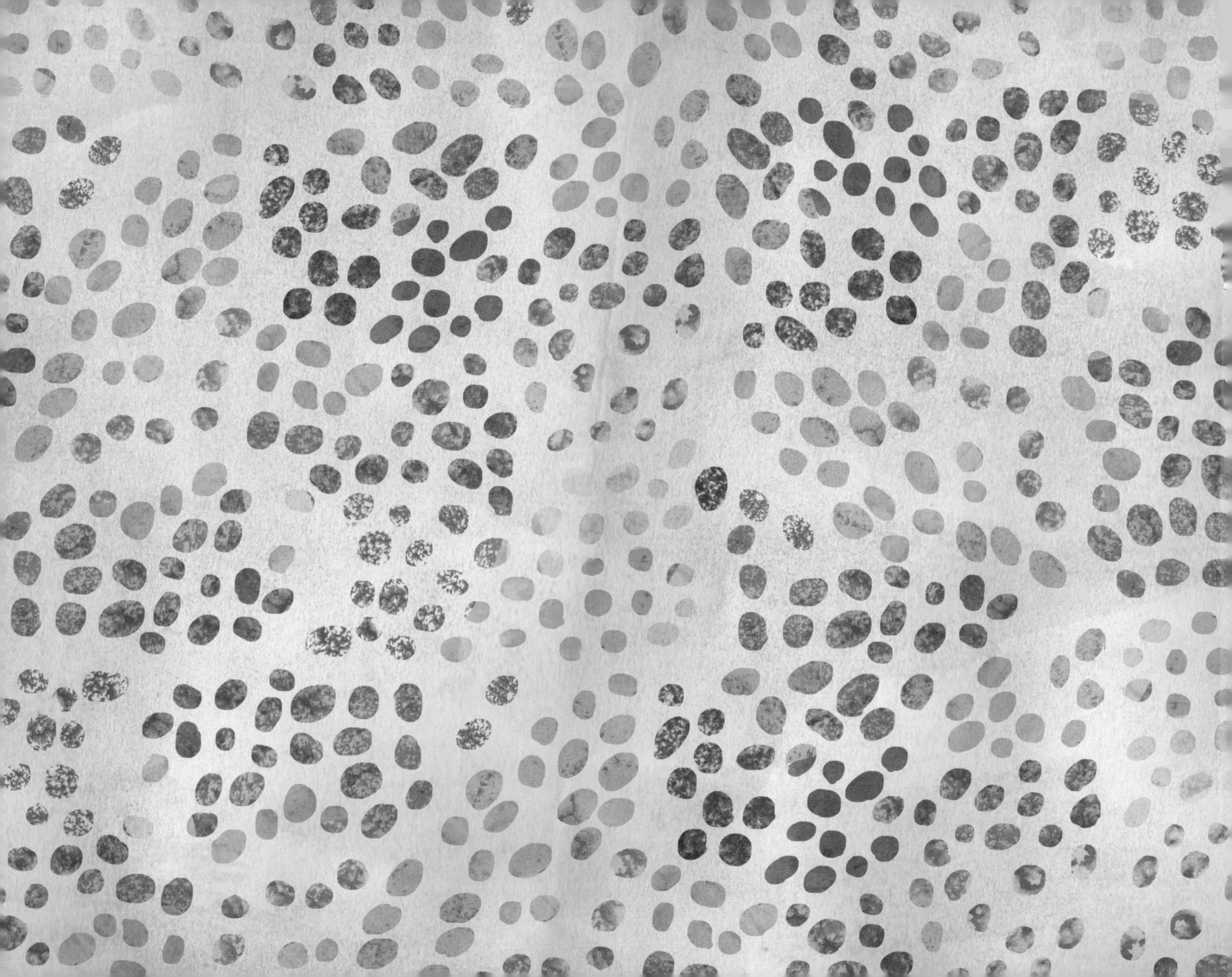